OCT   2014

My YIDDISH VACATION

IONE SKYE

illustrated by

SCOTT MENCHIN

Christy Ottaviano Books

Henry Holt and Company

New York

For Grandma Tillie and Grandpa Benny,
who always put family first
—*I. S.*

For Nana Rose, who always
thought I was a little meshuggener
—*S. M.*

Henry Holt and Company, LLC
Publishers since 1866
175 Fifth Avenue
New York, New York 10010
mackids.com

Henry Holt® is a registered trademark of Henry Holt and Company, LLC.
Text copyright © 2014 by Ione Skye
Illustrations copyright © 2014 by Scott Menchin
All rights reserved.

Library of Congress Cataloging-in-Publication Data is available.

ISBN 978-0-8050-9512-8

Henry Holt books may be purchased for business or promotional use.
For information on bulk purchases, please contact Macmillan Corporate
and Premium Sales Department at (800) 221-7945 x5442 or by e-mail at
specialmarkets@macmillan.com.

First Edition—2014
Printed in China by Macmillan Production Asia Ltd., Kowloon Bay,
Hong Kong (vendor code: PS)

1 3 5 7 9 10 8 6 4 2

Author's Note

My brother and I grew up in Hollywood in the 1970s, raised by our hippie mom. We led a wild and free lifestyle. When we would visit my grandparents, their old-world coziness was a welcome contrast. My grandparents and their friends had a more meat-and-potatoes kind of vibe—or, should I say, cold borscht and potato pancakes!

Grandma Tillie, Grandpa Benny, my brother Donovan, and me at South Street Pier in New York City, 1974

Although my grandparents spoke primarily in English, Yiddish words were peppered throughout their vocabulary. I never thought of Yiddish as a different language; the words just felt natural to me. I still appreciate Yiddish words, especially now that I don't hear them as often as I did while growing up. Although definitions of Yiddish words are fluid and people use them in slightly different ways, I've used the words in this book the way I heard them when I was young. Imagining Ruth and Sammy's trip to Florida, and remembering my own Yiddish vacations, allowed me to rekindle my love for this expressive language that is a part of my heritage and certainly a fond memory of my childhood.

Me dressed in Grandma Tillie's clothes, 1979

How Donovan found this crazy suit in his size, I don't know! 1979

Grandma Tillie and Grandpa Benny on a cruise, 1970s

Tomorrow I'm going to Florida for the weekend to visit my grandparents. I wish I could move the clock ahead so that it's morning already! You might say I'm on *shpilkes*. That's a Yiddish word that means "impatient."

SHPiLKeS

Yiddish is a Jewish language made up mostly of German and Hebrew. My grandparents speak it, and every time I see them they teach me different words. I love Yiddish because the words are fun to say and sound like what they mean.

YiDDiSH

Mom is letting me pack ten stuffed animals in my suitcase. I didn't think she would say yes, but when I begged and said it would be a *mitzva* if she let me, she laughed and said, "Okay." Sometimes she surprises me.

My parents are staying in New York City for their anniversary, so my brother, Sammy, and I are going to fly on the plane alone.

MITZVA

Sammy is thirteen. He likes girls and music.
I'm Ruth and I'm seven. I like to daydream.

At last we are on the plane. Far away from school. Closer to Grandma and Grandpa and all the other people who live in Florida where it's warm even in the winter. I guess they like to *shvitz*. *Shvitzing* means "sweating." Try saying, "I'm *shvitzing!*" It's fun!

I fall asleep before the movie starts. When I wake up, Sammy, who thinks he's the boss of me, tries to make me eat cold eggs. I say *feh!* and wrinkle my nose just like Grandma does, then sit with my mouth closed until the flight attendant takes the eggs away. Before long, the plane is landing.

SHTARKER

After we arrive, Grandpa meets us at baggage claim. Sammy tries to carry the bags himself, but Grandpa's too fast for him. Grandpa is strong, a real *shtarker*. He was a taxi driver in New York City for thirty years, so he's had a lot of practice with bags.

Grandpa's got big opinions. In the car he talks loudly about what's wrong in the world. "Benny," Grandma says, "stop boring everyone with politics, and pay attention to the road!" I think he embarrasses Grandma sometimes.

We drop our bags at the house and go straight to the club for a swim. I love to look at the swimmers and their *shmaltz* underwater. *Shmaltz* is Yiddish for cooking fat. Grandma jokes she likes her *shmaltz* because it helps her float.

SHMALTZ

There are lots of grandkids at the pool, and we splash and scream and act like *meshuggeners* while Sammy shows off his diving.

MESHUGGENERS

ALTER KOCKERS

When I've had enough of the pool, I play shuffleboard with Grandpa's buddies Harry and Frankie, and I win!

"Good game, Ruthie," Harry says. "Thanks for playing with us two *alter kockers*."

"Aw, you're not so old, Harry," I say. "I bet you'll win next time."

My grandparents' house has special furniture. The sofa is covered in plastic to protect it from Muffin. Grandpa says Muffin's a *lobus*, a wise guy: When you let him out the back door, he wants to come in; when you let him in, he wants to go out.

LOBUS

TCHOTCHKES

Grandma has a collection of little glass statues and boxes that she keeps on a special shelf. Sammy says her *tchotchkes* are tacky, but I love them.

My favorite thing, though, is the wallpaper in the bathroom. It has velvet roses and poodles on it. I like to touch them when I'm brushing my teeth before bed.

In the morning, I help Grandpa make Grandma's cup of coffee. "*Oy vay!*" we hear her shout. "This coffee tastes awful."

Grandpa holds up a box of salt. Oops! I thought it was the sugar.

"Oh, no," he laughs. "We're out of sugar. Go *shnorrer* some sugar from our neighbors, Ruthie." A *shnorrer* is someone who borrows without giving anything back. I hope I don't become a *shnorrer* when I grow up.

SHNORRER

YENTAS

Grandma and I go out with her friends for
lunch. They talk mostly about their kids and their
grandchildren. I think it's gossip. When they talk this
way, all the husbands call them *yentas*.

We're tired after lunch, so we go home for a *shluf*. Tonight we'll go line dancing. Sammy says he'd rather ride his bike to the 7-Eleven and hang out with the older kids, but Grandpa won't let him. He says those kids are nothing but *nudniks*.

SHLUF

"What's a *nudnik*?" I ask Grandma as we're
getting dressed.

"A troublemaker, honey," Grandma answers.
Sammy isn't a troublemaker, not yet anyway.

NUDNIK

I brought my best dress but Grandma says it's too fancy. She says I should wear a *shmatte* like hers. *Shmatte* means "rags," but you can call casual clothes *shmattes*. I don't want to wear a simple dress, so I think I'll stick with my nice one.

SHMATTE

When we get there, Harry and Frankie are dancing up a storm, so Grandpa and I join right in.

"I'm too old for line dancing," Sammy says, and won't get up from his seat.

MACHER

"Frankie thinks he's a real *macher* dressed in those clothes," Grandpa whispers to me. A *macher* is a "big shot."

I'm excited when my favorite song comes on— "Mack the Knife." It's such a great song that even Sammy can't help himself. He grabs Grandma's hand and we all dance together.

It's way past our bedtime when we get back. As Grandma tucks Sammy and me in, I think about how much I'll miss her and Grandpa when we go home tomorrow morning.

"You bring us such *nachas*," she says.

"What's *nachas*, Grandma?" Sammy and I ask at the same time.

"Joy," says Grandma. "You bring us great joy."

NACHAS

GLOSSARY

Alter kocker. [OLL-ter KOCK-er] A crotchety old man. Also spelled *alter kaker* and *alter koker*.

Feh!. A word used to mean "It stinks! No good!"

Lobus. A little monster; wise guy. Also spelled *lobbus*.

Macher. [MOKH-er] The boss; the big shot who makes things happen. Also spelled *makher*.

Meshuggener. [m'-SHU-geh-neh] A silly, nutty man. Also spelled *mashugana*, *mishugehner*.

Mitzva. [MITZ-veh] A good deed. Also spelled *mitzvah*.

Nachas. [NOKH-ess] Pride, joy.

Nudnik. [rhymes with *could pick*] An obnoxious nuisance; a pest.

Oy vay. [rhymes with *boy way*] An expression meaning "Woe is me!" or "Alas!" Also used to express delight and pleasure.

Shluf. [rhymes with *rough*] A nap. Also spelled *schluff*.

Shmaltz. [SHMOLTS] Rendered cooking fat, usually chicken fat. Can also be used to describe something that is overly sentimental, like a *schmaltzy* movie with lots of kissing. Also spelled *schmaltz*.

Shmatte. [SHMOT-ta; rhymes with *pot a*] Rag; piece of cloth. A slang description of non-fancy clothes. Also spelled *shmata* or *shmotte*.

Shnorrer. [SHNOR-rer] NOUN: A person who mooches off other people and borrows without repaying the favor ("You are a *shnorrer*"). VERB: To borrow something with no intention of returning it ("Don't *shnorrer* my hat").

Shpilkes. [SHPIL-kis] Literally, pins, as in "pins and needles." Feeling antsy or excited.

Shtarker. [SHTARK-er] A big, strong man, often boastful.

Shvitz. [rhymes with *pits*] To sweat.

Tchotchke. [CHOCH-keh] Knickknack; trinkets like figurines and vases that clutter up end tables. Also spelled *chachki* and *tsakske*.

Yenta. [YEN-ta] A nosy person who is full of gossip. Also spelled *yente*.